Dreaming of Rivers

By

Hank Dallago

DEDICATION:

For my father, Edward F. Dallago.

Forward and Up

Dreaming of Rivers

By

Hank Dallago

CONTENTS

Foreword

Purpose/Notes: This book was written for teens in the hope they find a home within these poems, stories, and blank pages. A home where they may hang out and feel comfortable, slip-off their shoes, get cozy, and rest awhile with their thoughts and emotions. It may be enjoyed by others, too, who need to retreat to a quiet place of their own for personal reflection and self-discovery.

READER NOTES:

Let's start with an understanding of breathing and using the blank pages included in this book to provide space for your thoughts and feelings on paper as you explore these stories and poems.

On Breathing:

I'd like to encourage you to begin a breathing practice. By taking some time out of your day to breathe intentionally, slowing down your mind and body to help regenerate yourself and become more aware of not only *what* you are doing but also *why* you are doing it.

One of the benefits of my yoga practice has been learning how to breathe. Breathing has helped me achieve mental and emotional clarity to meet daily challenges, manage stress and anxiety, and simply to relax. It can be done once a day, twice a day, or multiple times, based on what is happening in your life from one day to the next. You decide what you need when you need it.

Let's begin with an example: Take a fresh orange and hold in the sunlight. See how bright the skin is and look where it was connected to the tree. Smell it. Roll it in the palm of your hands – feel its size and shape. Peel it slowly. Smell the sweet scent. Think about what needed to happen for nature to make this orange. Divide the orange and look at the shape and size and texture of the individual slices. Now, taste a slice. Let the flavor of the juice splash inside your mouth and around your tongue. Swallow slowly before tasting and enjoying another slice. You could even imagine this is the last orange on the planet that you will enjoy. When you've finished eating the orange, think about how much better the orange smelled and tasted because you did it intentionally. This is much like one practice of focused beathing.

Preparing to breathe: Decide if you want to sit in a comfortable position with legs uncrossed and arms at your side or lie on your back during your breathing practice. You may keep your eyes closed or open. I prefer to keep mine closed. Find a place that is quiet, where you feel safe, relaxed, and free from distractions (including texts, calls, emails, etc.). Try to be as relaxed as possible. Remember, breathing is vital to your overall health. So, maximize this time for yourself.

Breathing technique: Once you're in your space, inhale a breath of fresh air through your nose while counting to 4, 5, or 6, slowly. Fill your lungs with air and send the oxygen throughout your body. Exhale through your mouth counting to 5, 6, or 7, slowly. Notice the exhale can be one to two counts more than the inhale. This is done purposely to push-out the used oxygen before taking another breath of fresh air. These are guidelines so adjust them to what works best for you. Start with 1 to 2 minutes of a breathing practice and work up to 3 to 5 minutes.

If you're feeling anxious or stressed, it may take a while to find your breathing rhythm. Try to relax a little and start again. When my breathing practice is off, I sit quietly and try to let go of what is blocking my breath. This can take a couple of minutes or longer. Take your time. Try again when you're ready to find your rhythm. It may help to think of a happy place or person or pet that brings a smile to your face to help unblock the path of your breathing. The more your breathing becomes a habit, the smoother it becomes. But we all have off days, too.

After you have practiced breathing for a few minutes and are in a relaxed state of mind, you may want to spend more time in this special space that you have created. In time, you will notice the effect your breathing is having on you. Like the example of eating an orange, the basic purpose of intentional breathing is designed to quiet your mind and relax your body. It may also offer you the clarity to take the next positive step in your life. Or allow you to "see" in your mind's eye other ways to solve challenges in relationships, accomplish difficult tasks, overcome temporary setbacks, or simply use this time to meditate. Remember, though, that it takes time to achieve the many benefits of a breathing practice. So, be patient with yourself. Like most things worth achieving, breathing takes practice and a persistent desire to reap its benefits.

The Blank Pages:

The blank pages found throughout this book are just for you. And for you only. This is your private place to collect whatever thoughts and feelings you have from either this book or from any other source. It is up to you whether you choose to share any of this with anyone else. Use these pages to write down words, poems, stories, draw pictures, paint, tape things that will help you and your life goals. In other words, use the space to help define who you are and where you would like to go and who you would like to become. Make it personal. Make it all about you. Should you run out of space, continue to express yourself in any way you choose using basic notebooks or journals. When one notebook or journal is full, start another, and then another…You can make this a daily or weekly habit if it helps to express your thoughts and emotions. It's another way to be true to yourself.

FOREWORD

In *Dreaming of Rivers*, poet Hank Dallago has provided not only a comfortable home for teens to hang out and perhaps create their own thoughts and feelings, but a place for all of us to enjoy some quiet time as we listen to his soothing voice. Sometimes his poems take the shape of an interior conversation. In "Promise," he asks: "*Am I to wonder out here, forever a nobody?* Your time will come." In "Bait and Switch" the poet offers a quiet meditation on flyfishing: "strange ballet in slow motion—/liquified scene in a distant dream." We learn much about the life behind the poet. The poem "Gardener," for example, provides a loving remembrance of how his mother tended her family like a garden: "patch a tear, stitch a wound, /clean a stain, bear a loss." While many of the poems are playful, such as his delightful "Ups and Downs" about yo-yo's: "a joyride with wings," others are more serious. In "Infinite," one of the more powerful pieces in this collection, he meditates on the pandemic and its relentless, tragic numbers: "some numbers are more verbal/ than others. Like ones that broad-/cast a daily tally of the deceased" and concludes "How a small number/of digits multiplied/life's incalculability."

Much like love, Hank is a poet with "an uncommon connection to everything."

Gene Twaronite, author of the poetry collections *The Museum of Unwearable Shoes* and *Shopping Cart Dreams* (Kelsay Books)

FRIENDSHIP RECIPE

Take:

> *2 people who want to have a friendship with one another*
>
> *1 large portion of honest humility and genuine patience*
>
> *2 scoops of spirituality…love in a higher power*
>
> *3 full buckets of maturing self-esteem, generously*
>
> *mixed with a like amount of self-love and self-acceptance*
>
> *An oversized bag of similarly shared values and morals,*
>
> *with added morsels of flexibility and independence*
>
> *Plenty of healthful food, water, exercise, and rest*

Combine all above ingredients and begin to care for your friendship

Add generous portions of openness and notice how your friendship

is starting to grow (as no two friendships are exactly alike)

Continue to sprinkle self-love, patience, and spirituality

plus, plenty of laughter to keep your friendship fun and exciting

Add kindness and keep your friendship close to your heart

Continue to change and let you and your friendship grow together

Serve with a side of wonder and share with others.

Enjoy!

CLARITY

I was the peacemaker. The one who wanted to be everyone's best friend. Plus, the overly sensitive one in our family. I simply needed to be liked and accepted for who I was growing up. I not only wanted everyone in my family to get along, but everyone at school, too. But I was bullied at school for being shorter than most and a person of color. My sensitivities were even greater when I felt there was a conflict between me and someone else. Naturally, I needed to fix it. So, being the people pleaser, with selfless tendencies, I would do just about anything to get people to like me. Because of my naïve personality the biggest feeling I had about my dad was anxiety. Inside that anxiety was a combination of frustration and rejection. It was the one relationship that I believed was broken and I didn't know how the heck to fix it.

When I began yoga at age sixteen, dad had already served with the Navy in WW II, Korean war, and later in Vietnam. With a penchant for perfection and discipline, dad was not the type to sit down with me and have a talk about feelings. Either his feelings, my feelings, or anyone else's. He was from a generation that served his country, worked extremely hard, and did what was needed to provide for his family. He was a great man in many ways, and we shared lots of family time fishing, camping, and other vacation trips. Though, as the middle child, my voice was typically drowned-out by three other siblings. And it felt like dad and I were opposites. He was working when I needed help on a school project or resting when I needed to talk about my relationships with school friends and especially the bullies. My sensitivity to his lack of understanding and caring were at times unbearable. So, I taught myself to play drums and percussion. Practiced yoga at home. Learned how to tell jokes to get the bullies off my back. But I became a loner at school after a third move to a new town in as many years. And though dad was interested in my life, he was also away for large blocks of time. Sure, mom was there but it was not the same as talking to dad.

Now, it was 1972 and yoga was not mainstream. Not even close. It was not popular or trendy and exercise classes were not commercialized like today. Yoga practice was in front of a black and white TV screen for 30 minutes a day. Mail order instructional booklets portrayed hand-sketched yoga positions; I practiced the poses on my own. The sketchbooks resembled primitive children's coloring books and consisted of about 10 to 15 poses. (Did I lose anybody there?) But here's the thing: Yoga became a source of inspiration to me. It was a connection I made early on like a seed planted deep within my heart. I didn't know it then, but it would take years for that seed to blossom and continue to grow.

Yoga began to take a turn and became my lifeline to being centered. I learned to find focus through meditation. Both yoga and meditation began to nourish me physically, mentally, and emotionally. That centeredness became a spotlight on my self-deprecating and anxious thoughts. I created a place where I asked the positives and negatives in my life to come together. Originally, I used everything in my power to have the positives win over the negatives. My goal was to create an understanding of who I had been in the past and remind myself of the person I was becoming. It was my connection to something incredibly worthwhile. Something wholly personal. Though my yoga seed was growing, the baggage it carried was a heavy load.

I graduated from college, married, and was blessed with two children. Though, due in part to my insecurities, my marriage soon ended in a painful divorce. I dove into playing music, work, and Taekwondo to ease the pain. To minimize my confusion, I read self-help books, listened to positive thinking tapes, practiced transcendental meditation, life-journaled, exercised, prayed, and somewhere in there practiced some yoga. Though I was still miserable I kept looking for ways to fix myself. Yoga was there to help me grow only when I made time for yoga. Occasionally I'd find solace with temporary moments of clarity when I'd desperately try to grasp its wisdom and remember its lessons. But they were like fleeting falling stars.

Meanwhile dad did not offer me the emotional support desperately needed. We continued to share time together as a family, but not the one-on-one time my heart craved. I had so many questions and needed them answered. Dad's unwavering response to my angst were that things would work out the more I worked on them. That I could do anything I set my mind to do and needed to work harder to attain what I wanted and not to let things bother me so much. So, the greater I vied for his validation of who I was and trying to become, the less he provided. Yet, I knew he loved me, and I loved him. But the bridge between us was as wide as the Grand Canyon! Dad was great in demonstrating discipline, willpower, ingenuity, strength, and confidence. He just didn't know how to communicate or relate to me in the way I needed him to. In fact, many times his emotional silence, other than his anger, was deafening. So, the bottled-up feelings of inferiority from past mistakes, poor judgement calls, my agonizing divorce, and countless screw-ups finally came pouring out of me like a fire hose.

With the help of counseling, my focus was back on practicing meditation, yoga, and drumming. In time my self-image improved as well as my attitude. Then something almost imperceptible began to shift inside of me again. I didn't fully know what it was at the time, and it wasn't easy to put into words. But with time and intention I slowly started to fit the pieces of my puzzle together. My yoga seed began to branch-out. The more I practiced mindful yoga the more I grew stronger emotionally and spiritually. I grew from the inside out. The effects were simultaneously subtle and overt. For the first time in my twenties, I felt complete. Alive. Whole. It was then that my relationship with dad changed profoundly. I finally understood he lived his life on his own terms, and I needed to live my life on my own, too. Perhaps that is what he had tried explaining to me during our "talks" together. It felt like hearing the maxim, 'when the student is ready the teacher appears.'

In my thirties, I understood just how significant relationships are between a parent and their children. The divorce left me feeling like I had lost a part of who I was as well as the closeness to my children. As if our relationship had been fractured and couldn't be repaired. I had the nauseous feeling day and night that since I had let them down as their father, they would not want to have a meaningful relationship with me. And to add to that, I was living in a different State than my children and hadn't seen them in over six months. Then, one night after a practice of yoga and meditation, I had a vivid dream where my children were now adults and asked me bluntly why I had not been a part of their lives? Why did I not make the effort and sacrifice to continue to love and cherish them as I committed to do as their father? I woke up from that dream in a cold sweat and within a month moved close to them to restart our relationship. It wasn't easy to do for many reasons, but it was the right thing to do, what I had to do to preserve our relationship no matter what! My yoga seed pointed me again in the direction of clarity and mindfulness to help realize how sacred family relationships are. It was also a time to learn a powerful lesson from my relationship with dad and carry that forward to use as a plus in my life.

Most of my insecurities have gone away. Should one come up, I give it enough attention to test its relevance and if it has none, then let it go. My clarity is what keeps me connected to yoga and yoga connected to me. My practice that began nearly fifty years ago is now about letting go and listening to what my body and mind need from one practice to the next. It's my lifeline to peacefulness, mindfulness, love, and a rare connection to life that brings me incredible joy. With a regular morning meditation and a yoga practice, I center myself with love and laughter. My incredible marriage of thirty years, close relationship with my three adult children and adopted grandson, all benefit from this clarity.

Dad died several years ago and with him a part of me went too. He had become my mentor and my moral compass. I learned so much more about his life and many sacrifices he made for his family. My respect, admiration, and love for him grew immensely. A few years before he passed, we had those long-awaited talks. Only then they were two adults sharing substantial life experiences with one another. We even talked about how much our relationship had changed and become better over the years. We laughed and we cried. And those cherished moments will remain in my heart forever. Dad had also mellowed, and I of course had matured. Though I once desperately needed his acceptance, the glimmers of love we shared made up for all those lean years combined. My yoga seed channeled those sensitivities into compassion and prayers of love for my family, friends, and community whether I'm aware of it or not.

In a serendipitous moment, while going through dad's belongings, I found a shoebox with three small hand-written notes of observations he made about me while I was three and four years old. Reading them lit-up my heart and connected my respect and love for him even more.

Scraps of Clarity

> There's a soul who wishes at times
>   he was not here but over there…

Well-hidden shoebox:
old letters   postcards
snapshots   drawings
on worn scraps of paper.

Wait…handwritten notes.
Few penciled lines result
in pershible keepsakes
of his observations of me.

Closer and closer we're
connected to the past
crisscross through time –
father and son homecoming.

Lasting comments I had not seen
musings compressed in timepiece
intersect to link a child
with a parent.

Heart-to-hearts unfinished
conversations interrupted –
understanding so clearly and
loving him immeasurably.

History of priceless impressions
extraordinary reunion of emotions
yesterday's kaleidoscope of thoughts
today's serendipitous deposits of joy.

WORK OF ART

Our spirited house in Flagstaff,
built by dad the year I was born
nurtured my first dream castle:
spacious rooms to trace open stars
hearth to buzz straight to the moon
wooden floors to brace rugged seas.

My sister Dolly, looks and charm
of Tina Fey. My brother Ed,
wicked smile and hilarious
antics of Ryan Reynolds.
Mom's macrame plant
hangings. Dad's harmonica to
hypnotize guests…for hours.

So, on my third birthday, as I shaped
my double layered chocolate cake into a
fortress with spoon, hands, and mouth,
dad shouted,

> *son, what are you doing*!

I answered,

> *this is my cake*
> *this is my birthday*
> *and this is my house…*
> *what are you going to do about it?*

I became the Michelangelo of our home.

LOST TREASURES

In 5th grade Jimmy and I were like a song and dance,
playing marbles at recess, after school, weekends.
We split jokes and snapped glances at girls whom
we nicknamed *Cat's Eyes*, *Ghost Swirls* or *Steelies*
after our favorite agates. On sleepovers, we'd swap
back sweethearts lost earlier then practice our sly stares.

When Frank the school bully cast his dark shadow
his cheating eclipsed the game
so, we switched to broken pieces –
pocketing our prized ones.

But in a forced game where Frank
elbowed in, swindled our darlings,
then thrust Jimmy and me into
a quarrel, retreated, shouting *Fight*!
kids quickly circled us
eager to hear a punch line.

After that sleepovers
stopped
plus, our sweethearts
and the girls were not
near as pretty.

ROAD TRIPS

Endless memories of six-in-a-1952-Chevy,
mom divvied-up cold drinks, soggy
bologna sandwiches, squashed chips
candy to outlast nonstop sing-a-longs
knock-knock jokes, burps, and farts.
Roadways never expected to carry stress
of four kids driven to find license plates
boarding states of Arizona, road signs
to spell nicknames, billboards for made-
up stories, listen to late night radio
stories. Dad stopped only if girls had to pee
leaving us boys to use a jar.
Since I got carsick, only taste or smell
of lemon or orange saved vomiting –
my pride from spewing into the upholstery –
family from spinning out of control –

> *Glimmer of lights peek over the horizon: drive*
> *to an air-cooled motel – head on a soft pillow*
> *asleep in my own bed –* aah! *long hot shower,*
> *dry towel, all-I-can-eat breakfast...*

Shortly, sound of street turns into a song as energy
shifts to greet our cousins, uncles, aunts, grandparents –
ready to serve-up homemade summers.

Dreaming of Rivers

16

NECESSITY

You both discovered innovative ways to raise
        four spirited kids   turn a 1960's dollar
            into a buck fifty:
rolled wooden dowels across a moist bar of soap
        to strengthen an armchair
touch of toothpaste to stop a lose hinge
        from crying
secondhand brush tape a steady hand
        for flawless paint lines
two to a room, two to a bath
        always six on vacation   meals at rest stops
           served in backseat of a station wagon
hand-me-down clothes shoes school reputations
        stretched like permanent plastic covering couches and chairs

'61 Buick upholstery, red on white
        vinyl labels alerting
           "Do not slam doors!"

Beyond the house, in the vegetable garden
        magic hair clippings protect buried treasure
preserve organic flavors of four adult children
        who crave a taste of necessity then (and) now.

DREAMING OF RIVERS

I prayed each day for rain
torrents of wet to wash away
the pain of a third move
in as many years

A high school sophomore
alone and afraid
surrounded by students'
torment of the new kid

Hundreds of single drops
crowded in lunchroom
isolated by pettiness
and indifferences yet
hungry for connections
like landlocked ponds
dreaming of rivers
flowing to the sea

I chose to share my lunch with tears
in a park with birds who were free

Thousands of single drops
thirstier than ever
hungry for connections
and soluble relationships
still pray for rain
to wash away pain
with drops enough
to reach the sea.

STILL

Scuba dive, snorkel, share
infinite blue with spinner dolphins
whale's humpback –
destiny of a heart
restless   searching

Heavenly twin sea and star
illume tracks
draw me inside deep –
spider's meticulous
unfurling of fleeting
lines

Submerged in island
songs by white crested whispers
liberated in rain mist
waterfall

Layered between me
and this world
washed by sea
stars and spider
as a swell of heart
finds
serenity.

PROMISE

Am I to wander out here, forever a nobody?

> Your time will come when you become somebody.

How will I know?

> When you and your emotions have a fun creative experience together.

But I'm new at airing my feelings.

> Yet in time, you'll meet the swirl of emotions that swing and sway like the wind.

Is it the only way?

> Yes. Listen. To that quiet voice when things are still. When heart and mind are open.

Well… what if… I'm not ready when it's time?

> You'll know when inspired energy pounds your chest and you must let it out.

Will I change forever?

> Only when you allow someone to take you apart, then piece you back together, will you become a thing of beauty – perhaps an extraordinary thing of beauty.

Is there anything else?

> Give yourself a gift of love every day. Then let it go and watch what comes back to you.

I promise to be my best.

> Then you are free to become… A Poem.

24

Bait and Switch

Thread spooled carefully through rod
leader line tied to a hand-made fly
woven and knotted meticulously
cast with an arc of hope –
fluid, soulful dance in the air
seize grand prize of the day

Scream as strike creases water
surprising myself from outburst
(rare in such angling)
my prize oblivious to my cry
ferociously working itself free,
while heart is caught in my throat

Second dance below the surface
one leaps in air, one grips the ground,
tango of two without breaking
tight embrace,
strange ballet in slow motion –
liquefied scene in a distant dream

Catch and release as my face wears
same upward curved shape on water –
both hooked from the experience
my heart back, bigger than before
trophy glistens in its natural state.

AFTER I BECAME REAL

*Real isn't how you are made, said the Skin Horse. It's a thing that
happens to you when a child loves you for a long, long time, not just to
play with, but REALLY loves you, then you become Real.*

—Margery Williams. *The Velveteen Rabbit*

Skin Horse made it sound possible
enough to believe every magic word
a fairy-tale dream held in a child's love
burrowed deep inside my thumping heart

Told love may only come after the loss of hair
eyes dropped out, turned old and scruffy,
enough time for kisses, cozy hugs, whispers
to soak into my skin and ragged body

Bunnies in the woods lit a different spark –
a different type of Real –
I wondered if another dream of love
could be a hop skip and jump away

Tail beats quickly when boy's outside
playing in the woods with another toy
feeling the secret place in our hearts
since Real love hearts beat together

Now my own bunnies run wild
through garden flowers with butterflies,
whiskers twitching, noses snuffling
in patches of meadows and trees.

And that same Real pain in my heart
when the boy got sick with fever
rushed in when my own was lost
missing, or worse, gone forever!

A lot can change in a rabbit's life
when waiting to find Real love:
a tear of hope to bloom a flower
special dust of a rare fairy,

and everyone knows there's sometimes no Real love without magic.

GREY SHOE BAG

When freed from their dwelling
dance in thin air as Beyonce and Jackson
ascend mountains as DiGiulian, Woods
soar and dunk ball like James, Jordan
scale uncharted waters as Cousteau
fish the deep oceans as Hemingway
trek trails like Skurka and Anderson
cycle the world like Sagan

Colorful kicks with distinct points:
high heels   to   sandals
hiking boots   to   sneakers
repository of sole mates
cloistered   crowded   awaiting

Perfect match to our endeavors
companions of swag or sweat
vagabonds to the uninitiated
stuffed together like sheep
weekend foot travelers playing the
supporting role in our finest feats
those enchanted warriors of souls

Cargo built and born to venture
New York…
          …Dublin
                    …Cologne
                              …Cardiff

Then tucked away carefully in
sturdy   stuffy   smelly   compartment
                    pre-paired for adventure
                              to spring   forward
                                                  afoot

                                                  again.

AIRBENDER

for Michael M.

You were in and out of crowds
as fast as legs would lift you
preferring to glide effortlessly
on streets with youthful riders
challenged to match the speed
and skill of a cycling avatar

bending   dimensions
force   of nature

clipped in your seat
like a race car driver
when decades of drafting
coasting and shifting
crossed a turning point

unrestrained as air
leaving this world
to enter another

        fearlessly!

SOUNDTRACKS

While listening to musical cassette tapes stored in
dad's garage, stretched from years of harsh weather,
instruments sounded as if played underwater,
vocals bubbling at depths of a hollowed-out ship.

My hope was to discover one in good shape
to cherish like an heirloom – dad playing his
harmonica – share it with siblings as a gift
on dad's passing of ten-years.

With an eclectic tape collection of country
pop, soft rock, blues/jazz, mariachi
polka, and indie – dad's musical genres
were as broad and lasting as his hugs.

I made sure to hear both sides as dad often
recorded himself in the spark of the hour,
on any tape available at the time, modestly
tossing it back into his collection.

Though quality of tapes were poor,
I played through a few – closed my eyes
replayed our shared rapture of music – pictured
his hands and feet tap, head bob to the beat.

I recovered a recording of dad playing,
though as expected it was not labeled,
it became an instant treasure, revered
with nostalgic pride, a musical gem.

Sensing there was more to be found,
I played a newer tape and altogether
overcome by a favorite titled:
How Can I Find Some Way To Tell You?

Dad Wore His Hat

like a badge of honor
bared a humble veteran of three wars
WWII (1939)   Korea (1950)   Vietnam (1955)
conveyed love of country – family – silent solitary sacrifices

random strangers thanked him
shaking hands vigorously,
my heart welled up with pride
along with a surge of pain

left my friends, my hometown
at turn of teenage years
to live on a Naval base –
never had a say either way…

      when dad enlisted a third time
      when bullies made my life miserable
      when I questioned if he'd ever return…
I understood his resolute confidence

he lived the Navy Seabee's motto, *Can Do*
to build paths to freedom
construct justice, build self-respect,
support unspoken weight his hat displays.

REFRAIN

I pause to hear a syllable
of your voice rouse my heart –

recall my favorite chapters
intimately worn pages
written long, long ago

Search for a solitary glance,
your loving face in a nearing crowd –

disappointment wearing long
upon my slow stare, then I'm
alone again

I feel your gentle touch
summon in the night –

distinct shadow crosses room,
lovely sturdy hands
caresses my bare shoulder

Embrace the unique scent of your hair,
skin, breath to illuminate memories –

imagine you piercing
through our thin veil
of separation

the pulse of your heartbeat
like pooled beads of rain –

rekindling a barren forest
blooming a desert flower
saturating a parched creek.

Sentinel

for Tia B.

Most mornings she walks
to the top of the hill
stands in the wind
     watches the waves
as spring smooths out
the edges of winter
flowers bloom near
     an outrageously blue sea
some days the sea is smooth
other days a mass of white caps
allows her to spot
     suppressed offshore rocks
imagines being with fishes
exploring that wonderous
world of towering
     pinnacles, waving forests
blue light filtering
above…but alas
she's not a mermaid
     she walks on earth
struggles with her aging
human body…
not easy
     but always possible.

GHOST LIGHT

A reflective look at 2020 when all theatre productions were closed
during the pandemic.

Bright as a klieg light:
searching a barren stage
exposing abandoned house
averting tragic accidents
exposing unruly spirits
sanctuary to exited
characters'
lone
act.

Light bulb
flashes to recall
performers' voices
animated expressions
emotions mirrored
in the audience
set in the
dark so
act
can
go
on!

To Unending Solicitations

(A prose poem to share humorously with a parent or grandparent)

I want to thank all the solicitors for their phone calls received recently. Their urgings and offerings have looked out for my best interest. More importantly, they satisfied that basic human need for peace of mind.

First, I'll mention those insistent callers who want to renew the extended warranty on my car, avoid a costly appliance bill, or provide a financial gift for an endangered species known to be extinct. Some ask how I'm doing, then assert themselves like the vacation specialists who phone at any given hour, day, or night, to reserve a trip a year in advance. Due to their persistence, I have a loan pending at the bank and arranged housing for my pets while I'm away on one of their too-good-to-be-true-once-in-a-lifetime-excursions! Can't wait!

Some warn that my social security number was used in a serious crime committed in South Texas. Why Texas, I ask? Predictably, these callers must be relentless, otherwise nobody would take them seriously. Yet, they find a solution to clear-up the entire mess (luckily, avoiding jail time) with only a hefty fee for me to pay.

They call to notify that my grandson was hospitalized and needs cash quickly. His name is not Andy, Elliott, or Pablo, and he's only five years old, not sixteen, but it's the thought that counts, right? Call centers often use foreign accents that I find intriguing, so I ask them to repeat themselves. Unfortunately, frustrated, they hang-up. It's another painful reminder that I should have paid more attention to my foreign language classes. And how so many people can work together in what sounds like a call center to assist people around the world boggles the mind.

I would be remiss not to mention the IRS. Callers threaten to seize my accounts and assets due to unpaid taxes, including hefty penalties. Imagine my shock! Luckily, once the sizable fee is satisfied, the FBI, Police, Sheriff, and local tax collector are miraculously called off the case.

Automated calls from Computer Services of America, American Funeral Services, and Reverse Mortgage of America get my patriotic attention. Call to stop a harmful computer virus, set-up a prepaid funeral plan, or borrow against my home. I admit to not owning a computer, will be cremated, and rent an apartment; they instantly switch to a credit card with an attractive one-time low introductory interest rate. I pinch myself!

SKIN DEEP

Shelter at home   vetting projects
repair disbeliefs rebuild promises renew hope

Five family members lost in fifteen months
one confirmed Covid but a loss   is a loss   is a loss

A trillion tears can't wash waves
of panic hidden in vulnerable places

Adhere to my careful list of duties
paint away pain   seal lasting stains

Quarantined from emotional quicksand
fear like wildfires spreads rampant

Uplifting songs blare from radio
news hour routs me down again

Ponder six feet wide, six feet under
no need to share a single word

Alarm sounds in the dread of night
wake-up gasping for disinfected air.

MANNEQUIN

Your fiberglass eyes
watch me try on
new clothing
with matching mask
that you wear on your
resilient plastic body.

If only you and I could
be more alike, beyond
our commonality of fashion –
concealed from Covid-19.

Like a perfect human
façade, you could shelter
every part of my vulnerable
body, avert permanent
harm until relentless
        vicious
        virus
released its bond on
        blood
        bone
        flesh
that can
never be
fully shielded.

52

INFINITE

Some numbers are more verbal
than others. Like ones that broad-
cast a daily tally of the deceased.
Or inform details of lockdowns,
mask wearing, isolation from friends—
that masked deadly trio.

Less verbose are the pounds I've
gained since the pandemic, hours
lost movie binging. Amount of turns
awake inside of night.

Then I obtained my ID—passport to
the second Covid shot. Emotions
dwarfed my tears. Instantly, infected
with relief, I soared home to engrave
time and place. Remind my skin
trillions of cells were protected.

     How, in one year
an invisible virus
changed everything.
     One minute heaven's
fading, the next
I'm flying.
     How a small number
of digits multiplied
life's incalculability.

GARDENER

Her bucket was usually full:

weeds, plants, flowers –

brown, crunchy like fallen

autumn leaves. Restored them

to the ground after a turn

in compost pile.

Tended to family the same:

mend cuttings

replant seedlings

nurture blossoms

bury losses.

Returned garden's gifts

on Sunday dinners.

Yearned for equal parts sun

and rain –

hope planted solace in her heart

in night's fertile soil.

Ups and Downs

Ballet of flair shared in the air
      two with wind in their hair
Teetertotter at each end
      bounce like springs when they bend

          Both add a hand-spin to their play
             in a round toss, pulling, winding way
          spin them down, then *freestyle* up
             get them ready for next lineup

Pull them taut for a *forward pass*
      make it look world class!
Throwdowns swing with a quick wrist
      faster up from a clever twist

          Circle back if caught linking
             avoid *flying saucers* clinking
          reel in the thrill with a big whoop
             show off with a *loop the loop*!

          Crisscross on a *breakaway*
             Leap in on *hop the fence* play…

Seesaw's a joyride with wings
      When yo-yo's pull all the strings.

MOUSE DROPS

Cap picked the ripest berries and peaches for breakfast while Kea prepared extra-dry toast to go with home-made apricot jam. Both then used the breadcrumbs to shape hearts for each other. One of the many ways they showed daily kindness to each other after their many years together.

On outings, Kea packed their favorites: crackers, cheese, watermelon, berries, sugar-coated almonds. Cap found the right spot where sun, shade and flowers nestled in a meadow, perfect spot for two mice to dine and dance, until the full moon began to flirt with the night sky.

Hot days found them at the rainwater pools, swimming, and playing "backpaddle," a made-up game to see who could float on their back the longest. Nearby he'd pick her favorite grapes, pears, and cherries. The long path home promised time to plan their next outing or prepare for the next season. She'd gather apples from a prized orchard to make his favorite sour-apple pie.

Cap had a habit of taking the quilt they "shared" at night. Kea made another for herself. Yet, by morning, both quilts burrowed around him comfortably. So, she snuggled-up close to him, saying it was to keep warm, but, of course, that was not the only reason.

When food was scarce as the sun, he would give her his portion to keep her healthy and strong, saying there was always more, but there never was. Though she suspected as much.

Friends invited them on magical getaways to the zoo, ocean-side boardwalks, and country fairs. They smiled, gave a familiar look to each other; saying they would think it over. Yet, their answer was always the same: *why leave our place in search of paradise when we have it here?*

One morning Cap woke up late, spoke in whispers, and moved like an unexpected dense fog. Said it was from old mushrooms or stale cheese. But after several days of averting her concerns, Kea knew what needed to be done. Leaving Cap alone for a few hours, she searched the woods for the special ingredients to make her Mouse Drops. This was much easier to do without him, quicker too, but it also was time to think that if her recipe didn't work what would she do without Cap. How could she go on without him? She quickly dismissed the thought. She boiled bark from a black peppermint tree, sassafras leaves, blueberry juice, honey, with fresh chamomile, mint, and rosemary. Cap sipped the drops each day. Kea knew her potion had done the trick when Cap was more chipper than a morning squirrel and just as talkative! It didn't take long then for them to plan their next outing together.

There were more outings, rainwater pools, gathering apples on long walks, quilt "hogging," tummy scratches, and afternoon naps. Although, Cap didn't ask what was in the secret potion and Kea said she couldn't remember the exact recipe, they knew there was magic in every drop. And just like their long lives together, it was her magic touch that mattered most.

FRESH PAINT

I scrape paint
from the wood trim
lining the sunroom.
Shavings, brittle and dull,
fall like a weathered
memory swept away
by wind and rain
to return to dust.
I apply a new coat
of paint to revive
a beautiful shine.
Quickly the trim
is restored to new.
How some things
cracked and chipped,
eroded by time,
birth a beauty
of their own.

Eulogy for Murphy

He was a cool breeze in a summer of Sunday's
reassuring friend in the dark –
calm you through a rough thunderstorm
lull you to sleep with a peaceful snore
ready to rain well-bred affection

He'd arrive on the throw rug as I'd show-up
on the page each day to write stories
where clownfish whirl, sea tides twirl
dragons ponder with wit and wonder
his mind spinning vibrant images
like in a land of a child's imagination

Our unwritten understanding was that he
would approve my stories and I'd provide
plenty of tasty treats to keep his interest,
reasonable arrangement till he'd fall asleep
then wake-up to reveal that fictitious look!

Black n' white photo adorns my office
reminds me how a rare night flower
leaves such an indelible mark
not only the howl in my heart
but the pawprints on my soul.

TOUCH OF BLUE

Elegy for Lily Dallago – Feb. 19, 1926 – August 25, 2021

You stood tall in my dreams,
adorned in a scarf, knit pom hat, gloves,
wintery boots to offer *me* comfort
while you were so frail, so fragile
only weeks earlier slipping
through my fingers

The younger-you would sit with me
on non-high school nights, liberate glasses
of red wine, wrinkle-free hands of thirty,
caution *don't tell your brothers or sister*
to cause your teenage son to blush

Watch old westerns and murder mysteries:
taught me to walk away or fight,
see through smoke and mirrors,
look square in the face of right and wrong

You, on a cold summer's night,
held me with your warm
stare until your brown eyes turned blue

I melted inside your arms,
pressed my head to your breast
      smelled your sweet breath   until we sighed   together.

YOUR FAVORITE COLOR RED

Barrel cactus uprooted from home
paired to mother earth
by a lone umbilical cord

lying southwards
clutching life with a yellow crown –
crimson circle of ornate flowers

Your flowered laugh, budding smile
asked for bouquets while living
then crafted beautiful wreaths as gifts

Extended your natural splendor for years
as you wished for the succulent to be
relocated somewhere safe…

Seeds will soon bloom summer fruit
a single cut landline returns to earth
urn's ashes will still tether an unseen cable

My displaced emotions will need grounding
while silent in my rooted thoughts…
I'll see red everywhere.

METAMORPHOSIS

You floated for a time
between each family member,
as you recuperated
part of you disappeared
with each move

crushed after dad died
then alone, after a broken hip
bedbound, hard to bear weight
you withdrew to another place
leaving us all far behind

more then less chatter
each time we spoke
like soundproof space
where your sagging smile
rested below squinting eyes

should have taken copious notes
memorialized like priceless
scrolls to be discovered
in a treasured cove
released like a choir of butterflies.

HAWAII TO YOU

*A*wake to the horizon exploding
with mango orange, papaya red
pineapple yellow – as jade green
waters pearl over your toes

*L*isten to laughter erupt from friends
a pebble's skip away, moments
ago were equal strangers, welcome
you to a groove as night embraces day

*O*bserve palm trees sway to dancers'
grass skirts as dolphins' spin
ageless stories, silky and soothing
as grains of volcanic sand

*H*ear tropical birds' chant,
hummingbirds' grant passage
to rainforests – while you lay
in a lanai midday to midnight

*A*bsorb the scent of plumeria
flowers, Polynesian choirs steeped
in ukuleles, guitars, drums to seize
whole islands' spirit in a conk shell……. forever.

Hank Dallago

WALES TO YOU

*W*atch the sunrise stretch
its gilded arms, *cwtch* you tightly, cast
sunbeams of an emerald countryside

*E*mbed yourself in a land
of people charmed and charming
as a community-tended garden

*L*isten to the spirited accent on family –
birth treasures instilled, endowed
generation to generation

*S*avor Llyn Clywedog Reservoir's majesty,
Blue Lagoon's alcove, Abergavenny's
culinary gala, Mumbles Pier's sea roar

*H*old the spirit of home in your heart –
retreat to an ever-enduring country,
lingering longer and reminiscing more.

75

I Bought My Wife a Father's Day Card on Mother's Day

not as a practical joke or to be foolish
simply because I forgot my glasses.
Though, it sure looked right
at the time through
blurred vision.

Admittedly, I bought the card the day before
but didn't realize my mistake until the next
morning. Rather than admit my blunder
I did what any self-respecting spouse
of three decades would do. Crossed-
out *Father's* wrote in *Mother's* and
set it atop kitchen table for my
beautiful bride. Bless her
she loved it, became
the day's headline
of laughter.

Still, I felt uneasy, not if my wife
expected another outlandish
card next year, but…
whether I would
remember
to grab
glasses.

LEGACY OF LOVE

Love will take you everywhere ♥

It shapes who you are today and who you will become tomorrow ♥

Love is a surrender to something much greater than yourself ♥

It starts in your heart and is with you everywhere you go ♥

Love is the only true power you have ♥

It's an uncommon connection to everything ♥

Love opens the heart to believe all things are possible ♥

It can turn you around in an instant or take a lifetime to reach ♥

Love is never too hard to mend, too small to lie hidden, too tired to rebound ♥

It can move mountains, change the course of history, and is the sweetest thing in life ♥

Love is always worth the effort to find and hold onto ♥

It is a shield, not from life, but from things in life that may cause you pain ♥

Love turns stone hearts into clay, forges miracles out of sand, and becomes priceless ♥

Love is contagious so you should spread it everywhere ♥

It reminds us of its joy through children's natural outbursts of laughter ♥

It opens more doors than all the other emotions combined ©

Love surprises – offer it here and it just may come back from over there ♥

It communicates beyond words and feelings, restoring itself through life and beyond♥

Love may never see the fruits of its labor, as the seed never sees its flowers' bloom ♥

Love is what ultimately matters most to our creator.

For Further Reading...

Breathing Resources: (Check first if available from your local library or used bookstore.)

Ultimate Guide to Yoga – Nancy J. Hajeski – Thunder Bay Press, 2021 (Introduction: The Breath of Life, pages 22 – 25 and 308 – 309).

Yoga Anatomy – Leslie Kaminoff – Human Kinetics books, 2007 (Chapter 1: Dynamics of Breathing, pages 1 – 16).

Yoga: The Poetry of the Body – Rodney Yee with Nina Zolotow – Thomas Dunne Books, 2002 (Observing Your Breath, pages 191 – 202).

Additional Breathing Resources:

Breath, The New Science of a Lost Art – James Nestor – Penguin, Imprint of Putnam Books, 20

Acknowledgements:

My heartfelt thanks to the many talented poets, writers, and friends who have provided me with invaluable inspiration and insight as a member of The Tucson Poetry Society. Also, my appreciation for the opportunity to expand my writing and reading skills as a member of the Arizona State Poetry Society, Society of Children's Book Writers and Illustrators, Tucson Festival of Books, and Make Way for Books. My genuine thanks to Sharon Skinner, Author and Certified Book Coach, who supported and guided me throughout this endeavor from start to finish. To my beautiful bride, Maureen, for her unflinching faith in every endeavor we've faced. And to my three extraordinary adult children, Carlo, Anneliese, and Ryan. Thank you for finding your own success within each of your hearts. I love you.

Author in HS, Circa 1973

Hank Dallago's first introduction to poetry took place when he was four or five and tried his hand at a written poem about chewing gum in an effort to follow in the footsteps of his dad's many romantic and rhythmic poems. It began a glow of poetry that smoldered deep inside. Though, it took another forty years for that initial spark to channel itself into a warm and cozy campfire, and at times, a raging forest fire.

Perhaps from being a middle child, prone to being sensitive and vulnerable, or having to face perplexing times in his youth, Hank has wanted to share what has taken years to understand and put into words. When he was in his mid-forties, Hank quit his prestigious position in a bank to become a youth director. For three years, he did everything he could to help make a difference in the lives of young people. As Hank says, "It's one of the most challenging things I've ever done and loved with all my heart."

Hank has practiced yoga, breathing, and percussion throughout his life. He lives with his family in Southern Arizona where he is learning to write other forms of poetry, the art of writing children's picture books, and new ways to express himself through percussion instruments and personal stories.